A Note to Parents

DK READERS is a compelling program for beginning readers, designed in conjunction with leading literacy experts, including Dr. Linda Gambrell, Distinguished Professor of Education at Clemson University. Dr. Gambrell has served as President of the National Reading Conference, the College Reading Association, and the International Reading Association.

Beautiful illustrations and superb full-color photographs combine with engaging, easy-to-read stories to offer a fresh approach to each subject in the series. Each DK READER is guaranteed to capture a child's interest while developing his or her reading skills, general knowledge, and love of reading.

The five levels of DK READERS are aimed at different reading abilities, enabling you to choose the books that are exactly right for your child:

Pre-level 1: Learning to read
Level 1: Beginning to read
Level 2: Beginning to read alone
Level 3: Reading alone
Level 4: Proficient readers

The "normal" age at which a child begins to read can be anywhere from three to eight years old. Adult participation through the lower levels is very helpful for providing encouragement, discussing storylines, and sounding out unfamiliar words.

No matter which level you select, you can be sure that you are helping your child learn to read, then read to learn!

LONDON, NEW YORK, MUNICH,
MELBOURNE, AND DELHI

Project Editor Caryn Jenner
Art Editor Jane Horne
US Editor Regina Kahney
Production Editor Marc Staples
Picture Researcher Angela Anderson
Jacket Designer Natalie Godwin
Publishing Manager Bridget Giles
Art Director Martin Wilson
Natural History Consultant
Theresa Greenaway

Reading Consultant
Linda Gambrell, Ph.D.

First American Edition, 2001
This edition, 2011
11 12 13 14 15 10 9 8 7 6 5 4
Published in the United States by DK Publishing
375 Hudson Street, New York, New York 10014
005-MB130P-02/2011
Copyright © 2001 Dorling Kindersley Limited.

Published in Great Britain by Dorling Kindersley Limited.

DK books are available at special discounts when purchased in bulk
for sales promotions, premiums, fund-raising, or educational use.
For details, contact: DK Publishing Special Markets
375 Hudson Street, New York, New York 10014
SpecialSales@dk.com

A catalog record for this book is available
from the Library of Congress

ISBN: 978-0-7566-7202-7 (pb)
ISBN: 978-0-7566-7203-4 (plc)

Color reproduction by Colourscan, Singapore
Printed and bound in the U.S.A. by Lake Book Manufacturing, Inc.

The publisher would like to thank the following for their kind
permission to reproduce their images :
Position key : c=center; b=bottom; l=left; r=right; t=top
Bruce Coleman Ltd: Jeff Foott 16-17; **N.H.P.A.:** 22-23, 25b;
Gerrard Lacz 2c, 6-7, 15, 28t, 32bl; Kevin Schafer 2b, 24;
Planet Earth Pictures: Ken Lucas 8-9, 32bl, 33; **Telegraph Colour
Library:** 4-5, 5b; David Fleetham 26-27, 29t; David Nardina 2t, 9tr;
Doug Perrine 18, 19, 20, 28b, 31, 32tr; Gnadinger 14b, 21t;
John Seagrim 29b; Masterfile 30; Peter Scoones 12-13;
Planet Earth/James D Watt 25c, 32cr2; S. Hilary 23 inset, 32cr1;
Steve Bloom 10-11, 19.
Jacket images: *Front:* **naturepl.com:** Brandon Cole.
All other images © Dorling Kindersley.
For further information see : www.dkimages.com

Discover more at

www.dk.com

DK READERS

BEGINNING
1
TO READ

Diving
Dolphin

Written by Karen Wallace

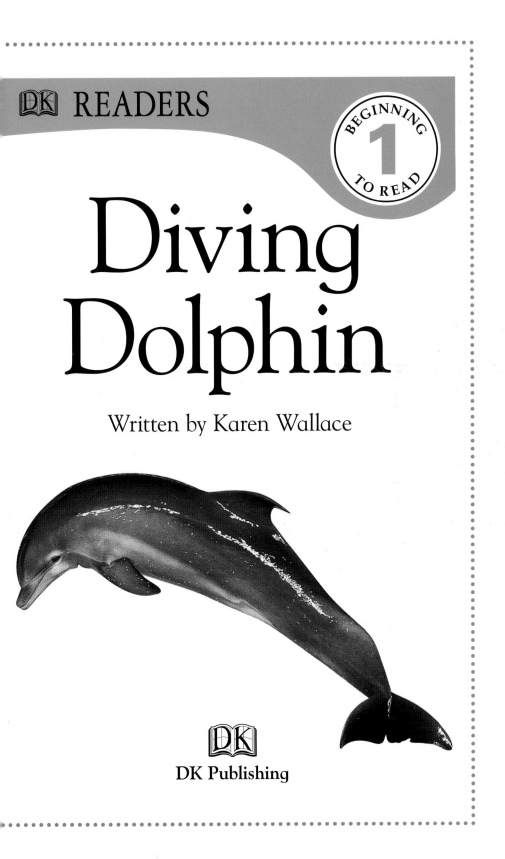

DK Publishing

A young dolphin
dives through the water.
His shiny skin is
as smooth as satin.
Far below,
he sees his mother.

His baby sister
swims beside her mother.

flipper

The yo[ung] dolphin beside h[is] mother. T[heir] flippers to[uch.]

The baby dolphin stays close to his mom. <u>This makes me think</u> she protects him and it also shows how they love each other.

The young dolphin twirls
beside his mother.
Their flippers touch.
They rub each other's beaks.

beak

Where has the
baby dolphin gone?

Mother dolphin calls her baby.
She makes a special
whistling sound.

Whistle!
Whistle!

The baby hears her mother calling.
The baby turns and
stays beside her.

The young dolphin swims away
with older dolphins.
He leaves his mother
and his baby sister.

He twirls and leaps
with the older dolphins.
They splash the water
with their tails.

Hundreds of fish
flash through the water.
The fish turn together.

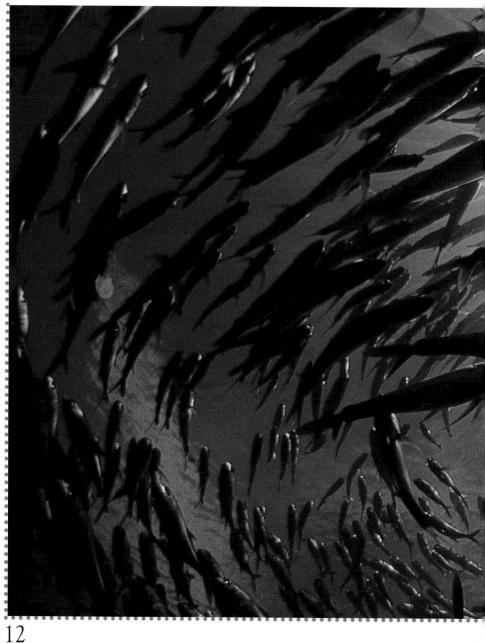

The dolphins follow.
The frightened fish
swim around in circles.

Dolphins snatch the silver fish.

Their teeth are sharp.

They gulp the fish down whole.

The growing dolphin
is always hungry.

He eats and eats to fill his belly.

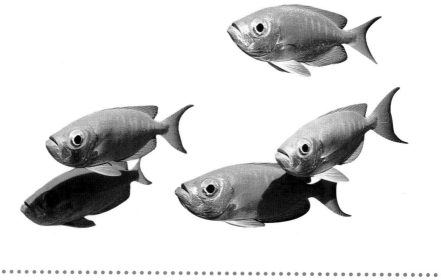

The dolphins turn
and dive together.
They spin and tumble.

They squeal and whistle.
When one swims off
the others follow.

The young dolphin
roams the ocean.
He hunts for fish
through beds of seaweed.

He rides the waves
to travel faster.
The waves push him
over the sparkling water.

The dolphin leaps
as the sun is setting.
The sea is smooth
and fish are hiding.

The dolphin sees the fish
in the water.
They glow like stars
far beneath him.

The dolphin chases
the fish.
He swims down and down
to the sandy seabed.

killer
whale

He does not know
that killer whales
watch him from above.
The killer whales are hungry.

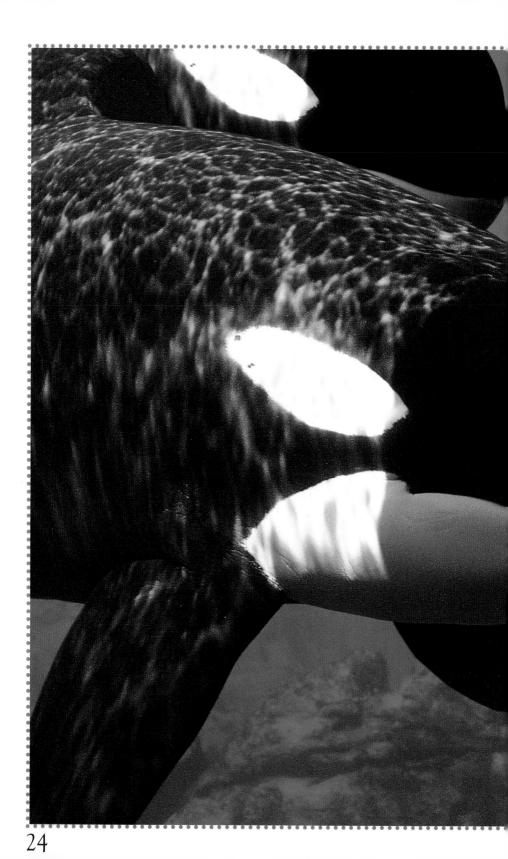

The killer whales
shoot through the water.
Their jaws are strong.
Their teeth are like knives.

jaw

The young dolphin
gives a warning whistle.
The other dolphins
race away.

The killer whales
swim through the water.
The dolphins hear them
coming closer.

The young dolphin hides.
He makes no sound.
This time the killer whales
don't find him.

The dolphin leaps.
He breathes in air
through a blowhole
on the top of
his head.

blowhole